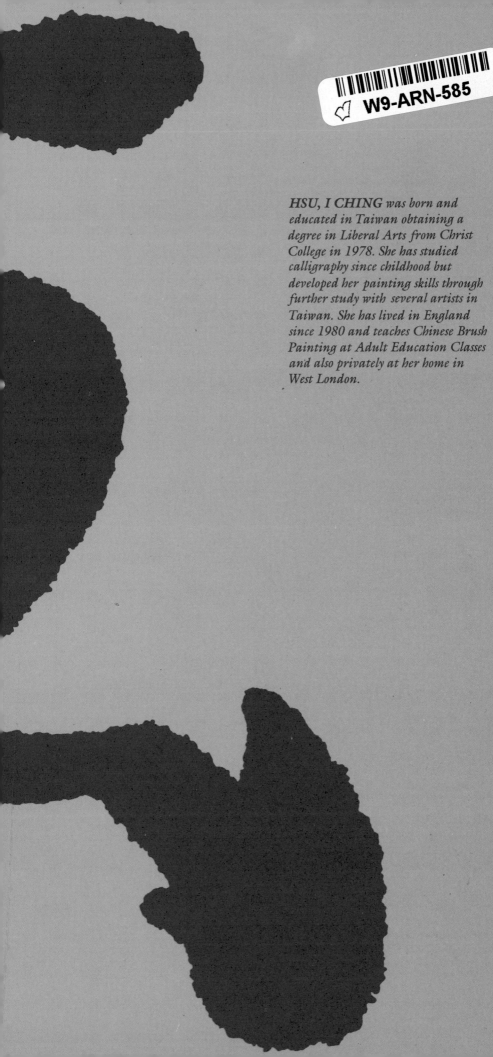

HSU, I CHING *was born and educated in Taiwan obtaining a degree in Liberal Arts from Christ College in 1978. She has studied calligraphy since childhood but developed her painting skills through further study with several artists in Taiwan. She has lived in England since 1980 and teaches Chinese Brush Painting at Adult Education Classes and also privately at her home in West London.*

Chinese
Brush Painting
WORKSTATION

I-CHING

WORKSTATION *is a new concept comprising all
the elements you need to start the art of
Chinese Brush Painting.*

*The first 48 pages of the book offer an introduction
to this beautiful subject with clear, full-color
illustrations. The last 32 pages are of fine quality
Chinese paper with which to begin
Chinese painting.*

PRICE STERN SLOAN
Los Angeles

A PRICE STERN SLOAN—DESIGN EYE BOOK

© 1993 by Design Eye Holdings Ltd.

Produced by Design Eye Ltd.

Published by Price Stern Sloan, Inc.

A member of The Putnam & Grosset Group, New York, New York.

ISBN: 0-8431-3753-3

FIRST EDITION

13579108642

This product is intended as a beginner's guide for ages 8 and up. Children under 8 years of age should be strictly supervised by an adult. Not suitable for children under 36 months.

Conforms to ASTM D4236-92.

Manufactured in China by Giftech Ltd.

Photography by Michele Rogers

CONTENTS

INTRODUCTION

*C*hinese Brush Painting is the art of using simple strokes of a brush to capture a single object or an entire scene. The Chinese have evolved their use of the brush ever since as early as 4000 B.C.

Painting has played an important part in China throughout the dynasties, particularly in court life. Traditional painting techniques have been handed down over the years from master to student.

Chinese Brush Painting is a fascinating art form and one that is within anyone's reach, young or old, whether you have previous painting experience or not.

Traditional Methods & Techniques

To take a course in Chinese Brush Painting is to get in touch with a tradition and method of painting that stretch back over 1,400 years. Against this historical background students have been introduced to a set of guiding principles that serve as both a foundation and a goal for prospective artists.

THE SIX PRINCIPLES

Collectively, these are referred to as Hsieh Ho's six principles and, for some 14 centuries, they have been widely accepted. To the western mind, it could easily seem that to follow such ancient principles is to sacrifice the very essence of self-expression that is so highly valued by our own art culture.

To the mind of the Chinese artist, on the other hand, the six principles offer the very framework through which an artist's individuality can be crystallized. To achieve this ability, the artist's technical skill must evolve to a high level before he or she is truly ready for self-expression. Only then does the brush become the medium through which the artist's inner feelings can be interpreted and expressed.

Hsieh Ho's principles are outlined below. It will be seen that the first principle has to do with the painter's state of mind, while the other five deal largely with method and technique.

1. The spirit of painting and rhythmic vitality

This basic principle seeks to convey one of the deepest meanings of Chinese paintings. The materials used are such that each brush stroke acts as a mirror to the artist's internal state. The quality of the brush stroke is therefore seen as reflecting the artist's inner vitality, sometimes referred to as Ch'i or vital energy.

Although a painting should follow the shape of the subject, it must also seek to capture the life energy. The shape describes the object's reality, while the life energy shows the object's vitality.

But can a painting show vitality? You have to observe every subject very carefully so that, when you start to paint, the strokes, color and composition will reflect the existence of vitality. By definition, this principle is the most difficult one both to teach and to learn. In time, however, as you begin to recognize it in the paintings of your teachers, so then you too will become more aware of it in your own paintings.

2. Natural form and structure, and the brush technique employed.

Brush pressure, turning the brush within a stroke and brush direction are all used to produce a balanced picture. No matter what kind of brush hair is used, if you can control the strokes onto just the right place then the best results will be achieved.

3. Depiction of a subject according to its nature, and the brush and ink application.

No matter what you are painting, the finished product in the end, must look like the object. To achieve this, you must observe the object carefully before you do your painting.

Once you have studied the object, you then need to choose which part of it you want to depict and which you are going to leave out. You must also avoid any unnecessary brush strokes. Form and space need to complement each other.

4. Color, and its application

The color doesn't always have to be the same as the real object. With the use of color, the painter can express his or her own personality as well as deciding whatever will give the composition a more balanced effect.

5. Composition, and the selection of subjects

In Chinese painting, the most common shape of paper used is oblong. When you are setting out the composition, you therefore have to remember the following:

- Do not make parallel brush lines.
- Do not make the brush stroke either too symmetrical or too similar— and therefore too dull. It is better to make strokes overlap rather than to give each stroke its own individual space.
- Space is always welcome. It is better than letting form become too complicated.

6. Studying classic paintings and copying a master's works

This last principle is about the whole process of learning Chinese painting. It is misunderstanding Chinese painting to think that the only way to learn it is to copy masterpieces.

Copying a teacher's work is one aspect of the learning process, but the most important thing is to develop your own. A work of art is a creative, rather than an imitative, process.

ASSIMILATING THE SIX PRINCIPLES

The skills and techniques covered by the six principles will all help the artist to create a painting that gives both the obvious superficial meaning together with a profound inner message. A painter must always have the rhythmic vitality of the painting uppermost in his or her thoughts. Only by achieving this will a painting have a living beauty that can arouse emotion in its spectator, who then becomes a collaborator.

Only when a student has become familiar with all six principles will he or she sense the intimate relationship that exists between the vital energy flowing through all forms of nature and the living beauty of their own creation. A good painting must always have this quality of creative beauty, revealing the spirituality of the painter as well as a mastery of the brush.

PAINTING
MATERIALS

THE BASIC CHINESE PAINTING EQUIPMENT you need includes: brushes, inkstick, inkstone and paper. These are known as the *Four Treasures*.

BRUSHES A Chinese-made brush is essential for good Chinese brush painting. It is made in a particular way so that it produces the correct strokes. These cannot be achieved with any other kind of brush. In general, two kinds of brushes are used.

• *A stiff brush.* A good quality stiff brush is made from wolf's or leopard's hair, which is brown, fine and hard. Stiff brushes are used for calligraphy as well as painting, and come in three bristle sizes—long, medium, and short. All bristle sizes are useful for outline work and for thin, fine lines and dots.

• *A soft brush.* A good quality soft brush is made from sheep's or goat's hair. Soft brushes are used for heavy branches, large leaves, flower petals, and for applying ink or color to cover larger areas.

*The two types of brushes used for painting: wolf's hair, **left** and goat's hair, **right**.*

A skillful artist can manipulate a brush to produce line and form that can be sharp, broad, light or dark, depending on the requirements of the subject.

For beginners, two good-quality medium size brushes, one of wolf's hair and one of goat's hair, are needed. Brushes made by Shang Hai Art are generally the best ones to buy. Brush handles are always made of bamboo. Price varies widely, depending on size and hair quality.

Using brushes. When a new brush is used for the first time, it will be hard as it is coated in starch for protection. To prepare your brushes for initial use, dip the bristles in warm water for about 20 minutes to dissolve the protective starch and then apply gentle pressure to soften the hairs.

All brushes must be cleaned after use. Most brushes come with a tassel on the end for hanging them up to store. Alternatively, stand them bristles upward in a pot after they are dry to allow the air to circulate around them.

Some brushes come with a cover to protect the bristles before use but do not replace this after it has been used, as the bristles will have swollen and the cover will damage the hairs if it is forced on.

THE INKSTICK The inkstick is made by impregnating gum with soot. Wood from the Tung oil or pine tree is first burned in a kiln and then the soot is scraped off the walls, mixed with glue and then molded into the required shape. The best-quality inksticks are made with the soot that is collected from the very top of the kiln.

Never leave the damp end of your inkstick standing on your inkstone after you have finished grinding as it will stick firm.

THE INKSTONE Inkstones are generally made from slate, which is not expensive, but they should be washed clean after use to preserve the fine surface.

Some inkstones come with lids, which can be used during breaks in painting to keep your mixed ink damp.

PAPER Chinese painting paper is made from the bark of the sandalwood tree and is known as Hsuan paper. It is sometimes mistakenly referred to as "rice paper"—but don't be tempted to use it for wrapping your spring rolls!

Chinese painting paper is very absorbent and it takes much practice and skill to paint on it. If there is too much water left on the brush, the ink will spread rapidly when the brush is applied, making it difficult to draw the shape desired. If the brush is too dry, on the other hand, it is difficult to complete a stroke.

You will need to experiment many times in order to become familiar with the absorbency of the paper and the effects of your brush strokes. The development of this skill is a fundamental technique of Chinese painting.

All these materials can be purchased at Chinese art shops and many other art shops.

Chinese painting paper comes in rolls or large sheets—some thick, others thin. When you hold the paper, you will notice that one side is smoother than the other. This is the side that you paint on.

In earlier times, before the invention of paper, Chinese painting was done on silk. Some modern artists still paint on silk but this material has a different kind of absorbency, making it suitable for different brush strokes altogether.

OTHER EQUIPMENT You also need a water tumbler for washing brushes, small dishes (old saucers will do) for mixing colors, an absorbent cloth laid beneath the paper to absorb any water that goes through the paper and onto the table during painting.

GETTING
STARTED

IT IS IMPORTANT FIRST OF all to learn how to hold the brush properly. This will not only enable you to develop a good brush stroke, but it will also allow your energy to flow smoothly onto your painting. This, in turn, gives more vitality to your painting.

The Chinese hold a brush perpendicular to the paper, both for writing characters and also for much of their painting. In *fig 1* you will see that your hand should be just below the center of the handle. The thumb is placed on the left of it, and the index and middle fingers on the right. The brush is then supported by the ring finger, with the little finger pressing against the ring finger.

When you are doing a small painting, you may rest the wrist and the elbow lightly on the table. These then move as the brush strokes are applied. When you are doing a large painting, both wrist and elbow are raised above the paper.

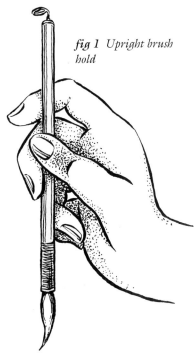

fig 1 Upright brush hold

How to hold the brush for different strokes. In fig 1, the brush is held vertically for powerful strokes. In fig 2, with the brush at a slant, the side is used to produce wider strokes. The wrist should remain stiff, while the fingers and arm do the movement.

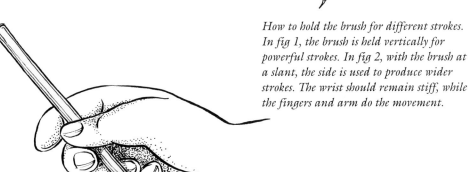

fig 2 Leaning brush hold

Basic Strokes

Once you know how to hold the brush, you can start with the basic brush strokes:

Upright holding brush stroke This is used for defining the outline or for doing dots and flicks.

Here, the petal outlines, branches and nodes are all thin strokes requiring control of the pressure used at the brush tip.

Different-sized dots can be simply achieved by using different pressure of the brush tip.

These bamboo nodes are done with a flick of the brush (see bamboo section, page 16).

Leaning brush stroke (horizontal brush stroke) Here the brush is held at a slant on one side and the brush side produces a wide brush stroke.

A leaning brush stroke can be manipulated to produce a range of effects by changing the pressure and angle of the brush.

With both types of brush stroke, a different result is produced by applying different and varying pressures, such as shown below.

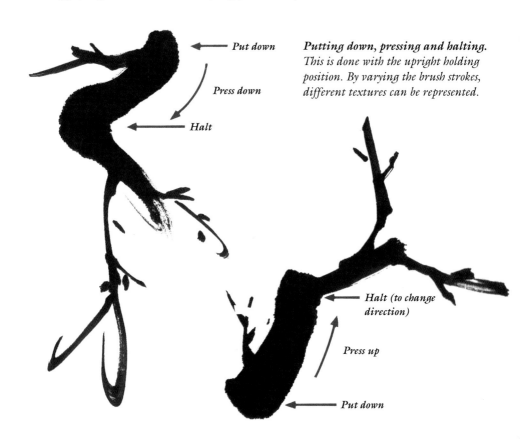

Put down

Press down

Halt

Putting down, pressing and halting.
This is done with the upright holding position. By varying the brush strokes, different textures can be represented.

Halt (to change direction)

Press up

Put down

Dragging and pulling strokes Each leaf is painted in one pulling stroke moving up the paper, using a different amount of pressure to produce the different thickness of leaf.

Reduce pressure

Increase pressure

Increase pressure

Press down slightly

Reduce pressure and gradually lift up

These long curling strokes can be painted in one section or two if another branch is added in one continuous brush movement.

Wrinkling and rubbing strokes *These are mostly used for painting rocks using the leaning brush hold. Your brush should be barely wet for the outline strokes and almost dry for the shading rubbing strokes.*

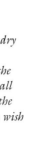

When doing rubbing strokes, you must dry the brush thoroughly and then place it sideways on very thick black ink. Press the brush onto absorbent paper to take out all the excess moisture. Then, lightly "rub" the side of the brush over the parts that you wish to shadow.

Tapering strokes *Using the upright brush hold, place the tip of the brush on one spot, apply slight pressure and then slowly move the brush in any direction, while, at the same time lifting it from the paper. Move the whole forearm for this stroke and not just the wrist.*

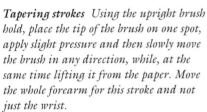

Pushing up/down *The thick line can be produced by using an upright held brush pressed down with most of the brush head laying on the paper. It can also be produced by simply leaning the brush to one side and pushing the brush up or down the paper. The thin line is produced with an upright held brush using very light pressure.*

All strokes must be made rapidly and without hesitation, from beginning to end. It is the fluency and rapidity of the artist's brush that produce the impression of spontaneity in Chinese art.

Through practice, the hand of the artist should acquire such familiarity in handling the brush that the mind and hand are left totally free to express their intention.

TECHNIQUES

Painting with Black Ink

In order to prepare ink for painting, first put a small drop of water into the sunken area of the inkstone and bring some out to the flat area. Then, holding the inkstick vertical to the inkstone, slowly use the inkstick to grind around and around until the ink/water mixture becomes sufficiently dark and sticky. Add a little more water on the flat area to grind again and so on. Never put in too much water to begin with. In Chinese painting, black is regarded as an important color in its own right. For this reason, you will see many paintings done solely in black. There are five shadings of black ink, involving a gradation of depth from heavy black to light gray.

Orchids can be painted in black ink by themselves but adding lighter shaded rocks gives the painting an added interest. Here the leaves were painted first followed by the flowers and lastly the rock itself.

Obtaining the different shadings is dependent upon the amount of water carried on the brush, as shown in *fig 1*. These gradations are used to show vitality, perspective and spontaneity in a painting.

SHADING

Shading via the application of the ink can be achieved in two ways:

- Two different tones of black ink may be applied separately, to show the contour of objects (see *fig 2*).
- The two different tones of black ink may be applied at the same time in one *horizontal* brush stroke, starting off dark and becoming progressively lighter (see *fig 3*). To achieve this result in one stroke, first apply the lighter ink to the brush and then dip the tip of the brush into a darker ink mixture. Using this method shows an interesting blending of light and dark throughout the stroke.

Study the examples here and experiment to see if you can achieve similar results. Understanding how to use ink to obtain the different shadings is an extremely important skill to master.

Heavy black To obtain this value, a dry brush is dipped in the ink.

Strong black A wet brush with the water squeezed out is dipped in the ink.

Medium black Place a small amount of ink on a dish and add a few drops of water.

Light black (gray) Use approximately half water and half ink.

Very light black (light gray) Use mostly water with just a few drops of ink.

fig 1

fig 2

fig 3

Varying shades of ink can be applied with each stroke as with the mushrooms here. The mushroom head was painted in one circular stroke of varied pressure, and a few light color lines were then added in the circle.

Shading can also be achieved within one stroke as in these leaves. Load the brush with a light gray ink and dip the brush tip into a darker ink. By using a leaning brush stroke, you can make different shades emerge in the one stroke.

Bamboo

It is very common for beginners to start by practicing bamboo as it incorporates some of the basic brush stroke techniques. Bamboo is also a particularly suitable subject for painting with just black ink and very satisfactory results can be obtained with just a little practice. Bamboo is painted with a wolf's hair brush in this order: stem, nodes, branches and leaves.

Stems *The stem is painted in sections from the bottom of the paper upward. The sections gradually increase in length as you move up and then become shorter again at the top. To paint a stem section (**fig 1**) place your brush down, move it up the paper and then lift it off, with a slight flick at the end of the stroke. Leave a small space (for the node) and add the next section.*

fig 1

Nodes *These are added in one brush stroke with a dark ink color. You can practice them separately to get the correct technique (**fig 2**). Slightly increase the brush pressure as you change direction at points **a** and **b**, making sure to add a slight curve to the line across.*

fig 2

Branches *Using an upright held brush, branches are added from the node at an angle of about 30° or less. Add them in sets of 3 strokes but avoid making zig-zag patterns as in **fig 3(c)**. The branch stroke should not end in a point (**d**) nor on the same level (**e**).*

fig 3

Leaves *These are done with one swift tapering brush stroke as shown in **fig 4**.*

*Place the tip of the brush at point **f**, press slightly upward first and then move the brush down (**g**). The last third of the leaf is gradually tapered to a point by lifting the brush off the paper (**h**). Leaves can be added in patterns of twos, threes, fours or even more (see **fig 5**). For all groupings, make sure the leaf tops of each set start from a different height and that the leaves are not parallel. A more natural look is achieved by overlapping sets on top of each other.*

Leaves can be added above or below a branch and you do not need to worry too much about showing the point at which a leaf is connected to a branch.

fig 4

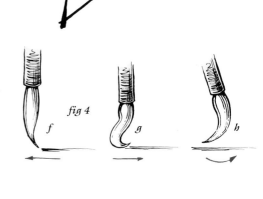

fig 5

Using different shades of black will add interest and depth to your painting. Darker shades attract the eye and pull toward the foreground, while lighter shades recede.

When several stems cross each other, avoid making them cross in the center. Make sure, also, that the nodes of different stems do not line up horizontally. Finally, remember that the use of space can be as effective as adding form, so avoid the temptation of adding too many branches and leaves to stems.

The Importance of Line

Lines or brush strokes may be long and thin or short and wide. Even a dot may be considered to be a short line.

The lines you leave behind on the paper—whether straight or curving, thin or thick—will all reflect the skill of your brush stroke, with no possibility of correcting an error. Brush strokes in your painting should therefore always aim to show softness and harmony and, at the same time, give the impression of vitality.

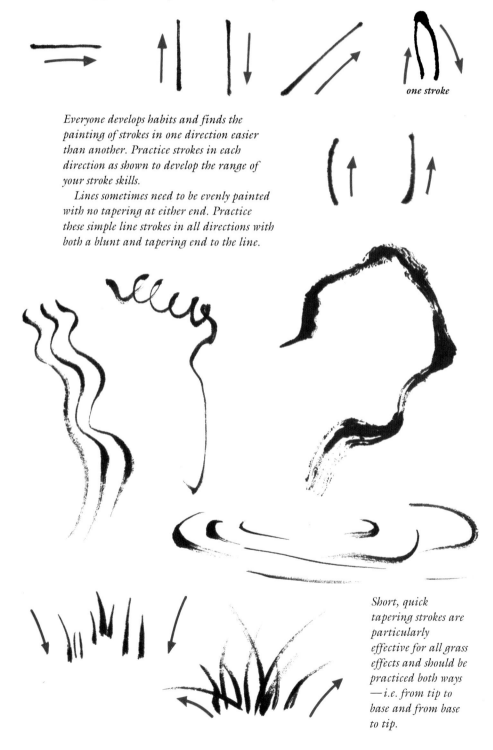

one stroke

Everyone develops habits and finds the painting of strokes in one direction easier than another. Practice strokes in each direction as shown to develop the range of your stroke skills.

Lines sometimes need to be evenly painted with no tapering at either end. Practice these simple line strokes in all directions with both a blunt and tapering end to the line.

Short, quick tapering strokes are particularly effective for all grass effects and should be practiced both ways —i.e. from tip to base and from base to tip.

Painting with Color

Given that so much can be achieved using only black, the use of other colors is in many ways an added extra. The following section will give you some idea of how color is used in Chinese painting.

The choice of colors in Chinese painting should be only those that contribute to an overall harmonious effect. Only one or two colors must dominate, while other colors remain subordinate. Do not mix sharp or bright colors as they will be too dominant in your painting.

Once the required color has been mixed, wet the brush in water and dip just its tip into the chosen color.

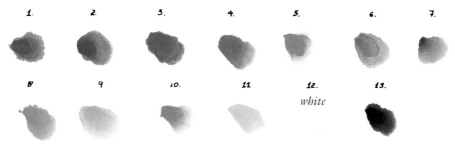

These colors and the various mixed combinations have been used in the paintings in this book. Whichever colors are chosen they must be brought into a harmonious effect. Colors can be added in one or more layers. Each layer can be added either when the previous layer is wet when you need the colors to merge, or dry, when you want them to remain distinct, for example when you are adding white veins to the petals.

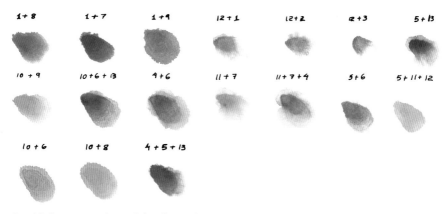

Combining two or three of the above colors increases choice enormously. Shades here are produced with the combined numbers as shown. For those not familiar with color mixing it is really a wonderful opportunity to experiment.

On paper, the first part of the stroke will show a deep color tone, with the lightest color at the base of the stroke and with various shadings in between.

To obtain the required shade, simply add more water or color.

In earlier times, Chinese artists seldom used white, as it was seen as a particularly flat color. Nowadays, white is used a great deal, and highly effective results can be obtained by mixing it with other colors. For beginners, the essential colors are white, crimson red, Indian yellow and indigo blue.

Try the following exercises to practice the use of color. Because goat's hair brushes are softer and more absorbent, they are most suitable for painting flowers or a big area.

First *put white color on the brush and then dip the tip of the brush into another color required.* **Hibiscus** *is done by mixing the white color on half of the brush then dipping the tip in red color. Start by pressing the brush stroke out from the center and gradually spread out the stroke holding the brush in a leaning position to allow each petal stroke to show two tones at the same time. Make sure the outer edge of the whole flower is not evenly painted. After the flower shape is formed, add in the white lines on each petal.*

Orchid flowers are painted with upright held brush strokes. Dip the white color onto half the length of the brush and then add a little purple color (mixed from red and blue) on the tip of the brush. The center two petals will be a darker color with the rest of the petals gradually turning a lighter color.

For some subjects, such as leaves, you will sometimes need to have two shades of one color on the brush at the same time. When painting leaves, using a wolf's hair brush is the most common but a goat's hair brush is also possible. Leaf colors are often mixed from yellow and blue with a little black or red added on the tip of the brush. When painting a leaf, both upright and leaning held brush strokes are used. Painting with colors in this way ensures the results appear as colors of different shadings representing a natural effect of sunlight on a leaf.

Plum Blossom

Plum Blossom can be painted just in black ink, but introducing color on the petals adds life to the painting. It is also a good way of practicing using a brush loaded with two different colors. Traditionally, only a section of a branch is depicted. Plum Blossom is painted in this order: branch, petals, stamen and calix.

Branch *The main branch is produced with an upright held brush —goat's or wolf's hair —moved across the paper with momentary halts to shift direction (**a**). The sections become progressively thinner with each change of direction. Side branches are then added, each done with one brush stroke until a balanced composition is obtained.*

*The side branches can cross or lie parallel to one another. Make sure they start off thicker where they join the main branch (**b**) and gradually become thinner. Small offshoots are painted using dark ink to show their vitality (**c**) and dots are added along the stem to describe the roughness of the bark (**d**).*

Blossom *Each blossom flower has five petals but some can be painted overlapping each other so that not all five need to be clearly visible. The blossom is added closely along both sides of a branch with buds placed only at the very end.*

Petals *Using a goat's hair brush, first dip half the brush head into white watercolor and then dip just the tip into red. With the brush leaning and using just the tip, draw an oval shape. You should end up with both red and white colors in the petal.*

Stamens *In dark black ink, paint thin lines outward from a central point, allowing them to overlap and spread out in different directions. Add dots in two rows at the tips but avoid making them into a neat circle.*

Calix *These are added with dark black ink to either the buds or to the back of the blossom. Use two or three very short, inward-facing tapering strokes (as if you were painting inverted commas) and add a thin center line for the stalk.*

PAINTING
STYLES

THERE ARE TWO BASIC STYLES IN Chinese Brush Painting. They are known as:

Hsieh-i (pronounced *Shiê-i*), which we call the free-brush method. Each brush stroke is painted on paper in a free and bold style. When an artist uses this style to paint a subject, he or she paints only the essential details by using the fewest possible strokes with color to present a free interpretation of nature.

Kung Pi (pronounced *Gong Bi*), which is stylized, and characterized by slow fine strokes of the brush, with the result being a precise watercolor showing everything in great detail.

*This lotus is painted in **Kung Pi** style.*
First the outline is painted including the leaf veins
and then the color is washed in. Lastly white veins
are added onto the petals.

*A camellia painted in **Hsieh-i** style.*
Here, the flowers were painted first and then the
leaves. Finally the branches were painted in but,
if necessary, some further leaves can be added
afterward to balance the composition.

Further styles of Chinese painting developed in addition to Hsieh-i and Kung Pi that include:

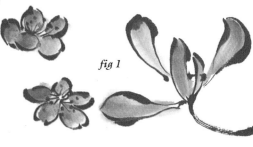

• *Gou Le*—Drawing the outline of an object and then filling in the color (*fig 1*).

fig 1

• *Moh Gu*—Painting directly without outline with color or black ink on the brush. This method is a similar style to Hsieh-i and shows strength and elegance in the freehand strokes of the brush. (*fig 2*)

When painting in outline (above and below), it is very important to develop control of the brush pressure as this needs to vary throughout the subject.

• *Bai Miao*—drawing the outline without adding color (*fig 3*).

A combination of the first two styles can also be done, which can result in interesting contrasts.

fig 3

fig 2

Effective painting without an outline can be achieved through developing fluency and confidence in the brush stroke, which is enhanced by the use of color mixing.

Chrysanthemum

This painting uses Hsieh-i and Kung Pi styles. The flowers are painted first followed by the leaves and then the stems.

Flowers *Paint the outlines of each petal using a wolf's hair brush. You can do them in one or two strokes as shown on the left, making sure you increase the pressure slightly at each petal point. Each petal is started from the center outward. Then, with a goat's hair brush, wash in the chosen color. Avoid placing the flowers at the same level or in a triangular shape.*

Stems *These can be painted either from the flower downward or from the bottom upward to link up with the flowers. Paint some stalks in a dark color to link up those leaves which are further away from the stem and as a final touch, add some small leaves on the main stem, using upright held heavy dot brush strokes.*

Leaves *You can use either goat's or wolf's hair brushes. There are two types of leaf strokes: holding your brush upright simply press it onto the paper or, with a leaning brush, make a pulling stroke. A leaf can be made with one or up to five strokes depending on its direction and angle. Make sure some of the leaves overlap. After the leaves are done, quickly add in the leaf veins before the paint dries out. (If this happens, add a little water onto the leaf and then add the veins.)*

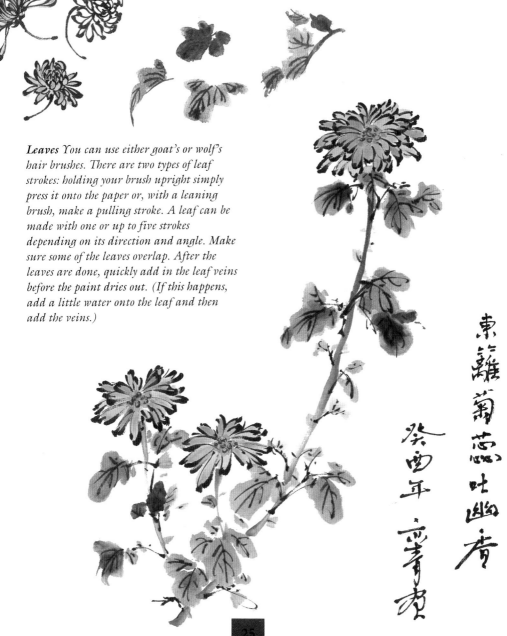

東籬菊蕊吐幽香

癸酉年 · 亞青畫

TRADITIONAL SUBJECTS

CHINESE PAINTINGS CAN DEPICT A variety of subjects. These are often portrayed on their own, but combinations of complementary subjects such as birds and flowers, are also very common.

Different artists suggest different starting points when painting birds and animals. Some start with the head while others suggest painting the body first.

Poultry

Chickens and roosters are popular subjects and they can be painted in caricature which adds a certain humor to the painting.

This rooster comprises a mixture of painting styles: line for the eye, beak and claws and without line for the body and bold strokes of the tail feathers.

The painting was started with the center line of the beak and then the eye. The positioning of the pupil can change the appearance of a subject and should therefore be carefully considered.

The tail feather effect is created by pressing the brush hard so that most of the black ink is discharged before the end part of the stroke.

Birds

Birds are ideal subjects to paint with a flower or a tree branch. It does not matter which you paint first—bird or branch. However, if you are adding a bird to a branch, make sure that you position it so that it does not appear to be falling off the branch.

The fuzzy feather effect on the body is achieved by using one or two strokes of watery brush and then, before that dries, using a drier brush loaded with a darker tone for the wing. You will find the wet body strokes can then absorb the wing stroke giving it a softer line.

In Chinese, we say "when painting a bird keep to the form of an egg."

Fish

The important aim in painting fish is to capture the poses of the fish swimming in water. In the painting below I have added a water background but it is not always necessary to paint water surrounding fish. The environment is suggested by the subject itself.

Painting fish starts with the head then the body and then the fins and tail. The body should be painted with a very watery light color and while it is wet, add white dots in rows for the scales.

The main body of the fin and tail should be painted first and before it dries. The lines in the fins should be painted with a slightly darker color ink. When you add the thin lines on the fins, put a little pressure at the end on some of them as if adding a dot. A horse's hair brush is ideal for painting the fins as it absorbs very little water. However a wolf's hair brush kept very dry can also be used.

These fish were painted with the orange-red crown first and then both eyes and mouth. Remember that with the fish eye, the pupil is always placed in the center.

This painting has a water background. The fish and seaweed were painted first, then a goat's hair brush dipped in clear water was washed onto the painting paper (not on the fish and seaweed). Before the water wash dries, quickly use a light watery green color and gently brush this onto the wet surface. The color blends into the wet paper, giving a very soft look and a natural effect.

Fish can also be painted with flowers such as a water lily or a lotus. In this painting, the lotus was painted first and the fish painted last. The view in this picture is looking down into the water at the fish. The lotus leaves and flowers are above the water but the stems are added to suggest that they are emerging from below.

Two fish are painted to symbolize a happy couple and this theme is repeated throughout the painting with pairings of flowers, weeds and lotus leaves.

Butterflies and Bees

Adding insects when painting a flower is a subtle and evocative way of suggesting its fragrance and the atmosphere of warm, summer days. Here, the butterfly and bees are emphasized by the composition. The flower hangs down from the top of the paper, focusing the attention on the insect.

The butterfly and bees are painted with the body first then the wing outlines and veins inside the wings. Choose the appropriate color and wash in when the outline is dry.

Butterflies and bees can be added to any flower painting. Place them in such a way so as to keep the overall picture balanced.

Shrimp

Prawns and shrimp are very traditional subjects and very enjoyable to paint. Start with the head first and then do the body in short curved strokes with a watery goat's hair brush. The claws are done from the body outward to the tip. Use a fine wolf's hair brush loaded with dark ink for the six feelers and paint them with one quick stroke in different directions out from the head.

As with fish, the subject itself and the addition of seaweed suggests the environment is water.

You can paint many other subjects in the Chinese manner. I hope the examples here will be a source of inspiration and encouragement for you.

Shrimp can be all facing the same way and placed side by side but avoid placing them in too rigid a fashion — adjust their angle to each other to make the composition seem more natural.

LANDSCAPES

ORIGINALLY, LANDSCAPES WERE USED ONLY as a background for the more important subject of figure painting. It was during the Tang dynasty, when many of China's arts flourished, that landscapes became an important subject in their own right.

Traditionally, landscapes must include high mountains with small trees. It is also customary to suggest one of the four seasons. This is done by drawing upon a clearly defined format, which gives clues to a particular season. The four seasons are normally represented thus:

Spring scenery This often includes large areas of fog. Streams are shown with a lot of blue, and mountains are painted with slightly more green.

Summer scenery Trees are full of green color and streams are shown as green with no waves. Clouds and a waterfall appear in the painting, with nearby streams, bridges and pavilions.

Autumn scenery For autumn the sky is given the same color as a stream. Some geese are flying in the sky and on the leaves of the trees there is some hint of changing color.

Winter scenery Much of the landscape is covered in snow. Fishing boats are usually shown parked by the shore, demonstrating that the fishing season is over. The water of the stream shows a little slow movement and there is a slightly sad feeling in the scene.

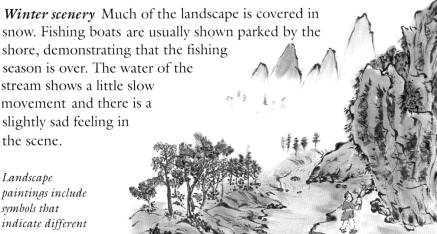

Landscape paintings include symbols that indicate different seasons. These two examples illustrate the scenery of winter and spring seasons.

When painting landscapes, some simple basic rules should be observed. For example, elements in the distance should not be depicted in detail. Thus, distant mountains should be painted without rocks and trees without branches. Similarly, figures in the distance should not have any features and streams should not have waves.

There are many different types of mountains and trees that can be included in your painting. In Chinese painting, the mountains are thought of as the bones and trees as the clothes. However, trees should not grow too busily on the mountain, as it is important not to make the mountain too messy.

Leafy trees should show a tender quality, while bare trees, with just branches showing, should reflect their quality of strength and hardness. In Chinese landscapes, trees generally have straight stems, unless they are growing from rocks, in which case the stems are slightly bent.

Trees on landscapes are painted in either outline or solid brush stroke styles. Their stems are upright when rooted in the soil or bent if rooted on the rock. Different styles can all be included within one painting.

In the following examples, I have shown how each of the component parts of landscape are painted but when you come to put them all together in your own landscape composition, do try to remember these points and I'm sure your landscape will be successful.

Leaves *Employing various simple brush strokes, lines or dots can produce very effective leaf patterns that give you a wide range of trees to add into your landscape painting.*

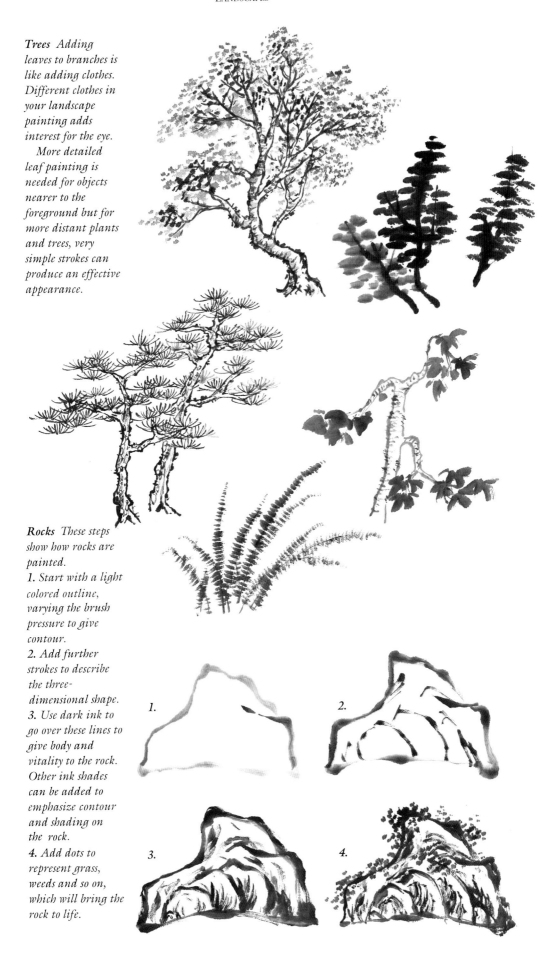

Trees *Adding leaves to branches is like adding clothes. Different clothes in your landscape painting adds interest for the eye.*

More detailed leaf painting is needed for objects nearer to the foreground but for more distant plants and trees, very simple strokes can produce an effective appearance.

Rocks *These steps show how rocks are painted.*
1. Start with a light colored outline, varying the brush pressure to give contour.
2. Add further strokes to describe the three-dimensional shape.
3. Use dark ink to go over these lines to give body and vitality to the rock. Other ink shades can be added to emphasize contour and shading on the rock.
4. Add dots to represent grass, weeds and so on, which will bring the rock to life.

1.

2.

3.

4.

Rock Formations

Group together the basic rock shape so that combinations of different rock sizes make an interesting formation.

Here, patterns 1, 2 and 4 can be placed in the lower part of your painting. Pattern 3 is of mountain shapes, which can only be placed in the distance in your painting. Pattern 4 is commonly placed by a river bank.

Water Formations

Water strokes are added after the rocks are finished.

Fine lines are used to show the movement of water flow. The movement effect comes mostly from painting curved lines on streams and straight lines on waterfalls. These lines should be finely painted in quickly executed single strokes. Wash the color in after all the black line work has been done.

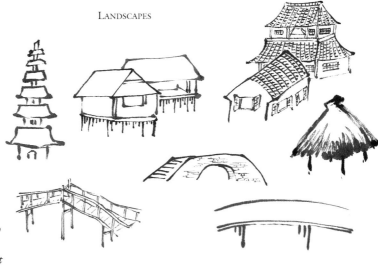

Buildings and bridges *Landscape painting needs to include the human element in some format. This can be a man-made object such as a building, a bridge or a boat.*

If placing more than one building in the landscape, do not set them in a row but put them at angles to each other.

Boats *Only simple style boats are used and, as with buildings and bridges, they need to be in a Chinese style.*

Figures *Figures are placed at some distance on landscapes and it is seldom that face details are added, as these are not seen as necessary. Again, the clothes are traditional Chinese style. Figures should not dominate the landscape as it is important that the human form is not seen to represent something larger than nature itself.*

When you have painted the outline of all the subjects on paper, you must wait for this to dry first before you proceed to wash in any color or another shade of black. Some subjects in the landscape can be quite complex and it is important to let each stage of the subject dry before adding the next shade or color.

If you make a mistake in the shade of black or the color that you put on the paper, you can still adjust it slightly so long as you do so before the wet paint dries. Adding color or different shades of black to your landscape painting will help create interest, contour and a sense of distance in the painting.

Step by Step Landscape: "Visiting Friends in the Spring"

In this landscape, I have used a light color wash on the mountains and water. Pink and orange flowers are added to indicate springtime. Misty mountains are also a symbol of spring in a landscape painting. Balance of composition is obtained here by setting the detailed trees, etc., on the left-hand side of the painting, with the bridge and boat on the right-hand side. A further balancing is achieved by the bright colored clothes worn by the boat figure.

step 1

step 2

Step 1.

The foreground is painted first, using light-colored ink. Start with the banks, the tree stems, the bridge and then the mountain outline.

Step 2.

Using darker ink, go over the outline again to add contrast. Increase brush pressure, especially on the bends of the outline. Further strokes are then added to the trees, giving a slight bend to the tree branches to suggest a wind movement.

Finishing the painting Using a wet brush, choose the required color to paint in all the objects. Leave some space on the mountain for the fog effect to be shown. Fog should be shown between the different sets of mountains and between the tree line and mountains to suggest distance. Fog effect is achieved by brushing clear water onto the paper and, before it dries, gently brushing on a white color. This will then spread out naturally leaving an uneven edge. A water effect is done in the same way using a light blue color.

CALLIGRAPHY

CHINESE PAINTING IS VERY DIFFERENT from any other kind of painting, as the skills it employs have their origins in calligraphy. Together, painting and calligraphy are referred to as the Twin Sisters.

Calligraphy is used on paintings for two reasons. One is to add the painter's signature and date. In addition, painters often add a poem that relates to the subject or feeling of the painting.

Writing Chinese calligraphy may seem like a daunting task, but it is worth persevering.

In learning the strokes of calligraphy, you will have an excellent training exercise for practicing the brush stroke techniques of Chinese brush painting.

Secondly, you may be able to obtain a Chinese name for yourself from a Chinese-speaking friend. It's quite common for westerners to be given a Chinese name based on the phonetics of their own name. If this is possible for you, you will then have at least three characters to practice so that you can sign your own work!

Basic Strokes

The first thing to remember when doing calligraphy is to grind up your ink to make it sufficiently black.

From the calligraphic point of view, the Chinese characters are all reduced into simple strokes.

There are nine strokes in theory and about seventeen in practice as shown here.

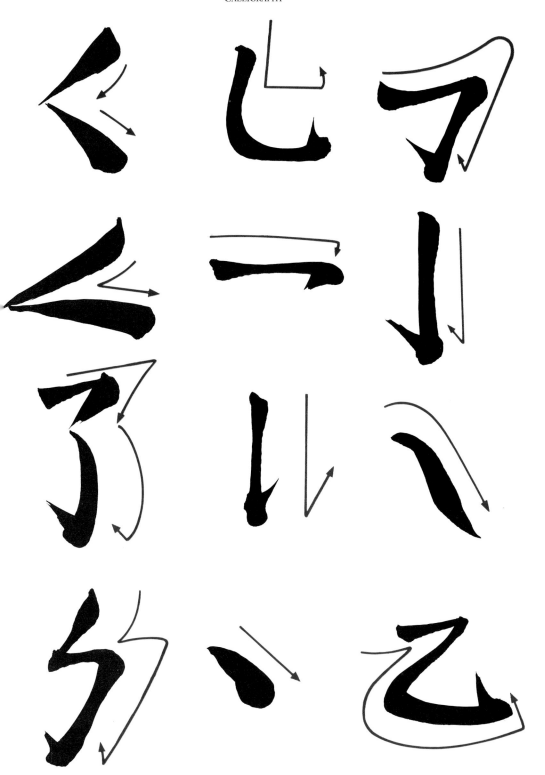

The main calligraphy strokes are shown here. As they are very specific and need to be executed with precision, you should practice them first, before going on to paint characters. The arrows indicate the movement of the brush as the strokes are carried out.

Wolf's or leopard's hair brushes are used for calligraphy and the brush is always held upright. The brush pressure varies depending on which direction the stroke tapers. For each character, there is a particular order by which the strokes are added—i.e. from left to right and from top to bottom. Most strokes include a flick of the brush at the end and this should be done slowly in order to obtain a nice finishing point.

Chinese Characters

In order to get the proportions of the character correct, it is best to practice on a square divided up into nine equal smaller squares.

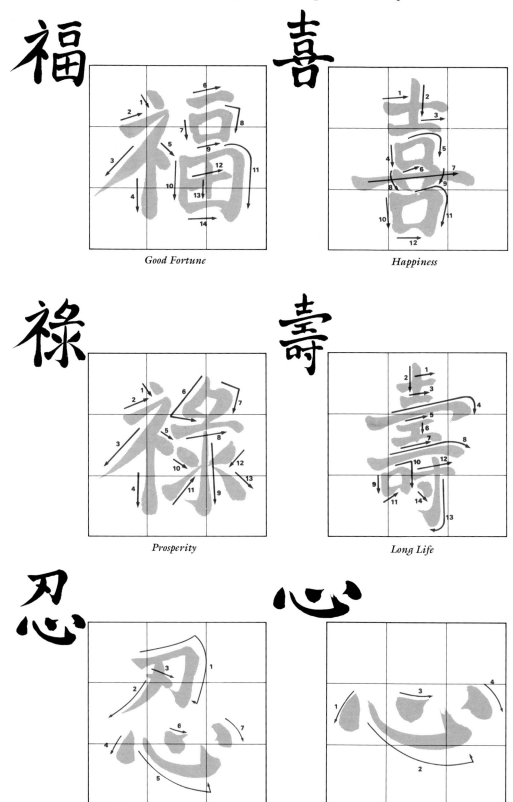

Good Fortune

Happiness

Prosperity

Long Life

Patience

Heart

生日快樂

如意

吉祥

聖誕快樂

Happy Birthday   *Good Luck*   *Peacefulness*   *Merry Christmas*

Poems

Poems are added as a finishing touch to a painting. Here are some which you can copy in your painting.

其性剛直

梅開五福

美人香草

菊蕊吐幽香

Bamboo
"Bamboo grows straight and strong"
Being hollow gives the bamboo a great resilience, it has tremendous strength and yet it can bend without breaking, a quality reflecting the deeper virtues found in the Chinese Philosophy of Taoism.

Plum Blossom
"Five good fortunes arrive when the plum blossom opens."
The five petals of the plum blossom flower symbolize, for the Chinese, the five good fortunes of longevity, wealth, health, love of virtue and natural death.

Orchid
"Fragrant Beauty"
The elegance, scent and beauty of the orchid are all captured in this simple poem. The imagery is of course chosen as an analogy to a description of a beautiful woman.

Chrysanthemum
"The Flowering Chrysanthemum sends out its scent."
The chrysanthemum grows upright and proud and its scent can be enjoyed from some distance. These qualities symbolize the virtuous aspects of a people growing upright, proud and with influence.

COMPOSITION

Whenyou are composing your painting, it is important to consider the proportions of space and form that the finished painting will have. As a general rule, a painting should be about one-third form and two-thirds space. It is important to seek a balance between form and space which reflects their interdependence. Between the form and the paper border, more space should be given above the painting than below, so as to reflect the space of heaven above and the earth below.

Paintings often look most effective because of their simplicity, so try not to overfill your painting. Your choice of color can also have an important effect on the overall balance of your painting and colors must therefore complement each other. Some subjects can complement each other if they are painted together, such as birds and flowers; flowers and butterflies; rocks and streams.

洋蘭

亦青己巳年畫

*In this painting, the strokes for the
orchid stem and leaves are kept as
simple as possible and this helps to
emphasize the more detailed painting
of the flower itself.*

The best way to develop your skills at composition is to copy other
paintings. Traditionally, teachers would encourage their students to copy
the work of old masters. On a practical note, though, you should feel
free to copy any painting to which you have access. By following this
procedure, you will not only be making a mechanical imitation, but it
will also help you understand and develop the skills of the painters of
these older works of art.

When copying another painter's work you can choose any of
three ways:

- You can reproduce the painting entirely—strokes, composition and
  colors. This may be useful to the beginner.
- You can copy just a portion of the painting.
- With added experience, you can pick and choose the several different
  component parts of several different paintings in order to combine
  them into a new painting. This last step will usually help the beginner
  to learn more about composition.

In addition to developing your skills by copying other painters, I want to encourage you to look to the many other sources and directions where you can find inspiration. From this wealth of material, the medium of Chinese brush painting offers a wonderful opportunity to express your innermost feelings in a painting filled with rhythm, spontaneity and living beauty.

Here, the bamboo is painted with a minimum of strokes. Economic brush strokes and the use of space produce a simple but harmonious balance with the form.

FINISHING TOUCHES

THE FINAL TOUCH TO THE painting itself is when a painter adds his or her seal to the painting. If you are able to find a Chinese name for yourself, it is quite possible to have a seal made for stamping on your finished work. Most "Chinatowns" have shops that will make a seal.

Seals are carved from the flat surface of a variety of materials. Here, the author's name is shown in three different scripts. You can also have a greeting carved—the seal on the far right is the Chinese character for "double happiness."

Framing

Chinese painting paper is very thin and it is necessary to put a backing behind it after a painting is done. This process is called "pasting." The simple way to paste a Chinese Painting is as follows:

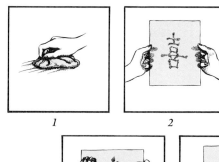

1

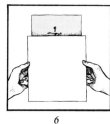

2

3

4

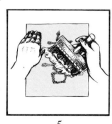

5

6

7

1. Prepare and polish a clean and flat surface, either a table or a board. 2. Place the painting face down on the work surface. 3. Prepare the glue. A good water-soluble paper glue is needed for this. Mix one-third paste with two-thirds water in a bowl until it is thoroughly mixed together. 4. The type of brush needed for this must have short, soft hair and be very firm. Wash the brush first and then squeeze away all excess water before use.

5. Very gently brush a thin layer of glue on to the back of the painting, taking care not to tear the very thin paper. You should always start brushing the glue on from the center of the painting, moving slowly toward each corner. Do practice this several times on discarded pieces of paper before you try it out on your cherished painting! 6. Prepare a piece of white cartridge paper or mounting card slightly larger than the size of the painting. Press the card on to the pasted painting, making sure that you press down evenly over all areas. 7. After a few minutes, turn the work over so that it is right side up. With a dry brush, carefully smooth away any air bubbles and then leave it to dry, ready for framing.

Like any other painting, your work will always be enhanced by choosing a suitable mounting board and frame. Smaller pieces of work can be mounted on blank cards, suitable for all occasions.

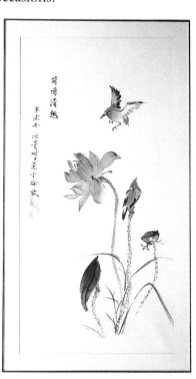

You will obviously have devoted some time to your painting, so make sure it is displayed to its best advantage. Here is some of my work, mounted onto cards and picture frames. The "Lotus and Bird" on the right is loaned courtesy of Chinn Hoffman.

CONCLUSION

美人香草

*I*n writing this book, it is my greatest wish that you will practice the ideas and techniques discussed and, having done so, will produce a painting that gives you lasting pleasure.

However, the pleasure of Chinese brush painting does not lie only in the finished product. It lies, too, in the presence of mind needed for each and every brush stroke. If the simple harmony in a Chinese painting is to be found, it will be because of the good foundations of the brush stroke. Appreciation of Chinese paintings is based as much on the brush strokes as it is on the finished composition itself. Of course, this is particularly the case in calligraphy which, for the Chinese, is an art form in itself.

The pleasure one obtains from practicing Chinese brush painting does not, therefore, rest only on the completion of a painting but can also be found in each and every brush stroke.

I do hope you find both enjoyment and pleasure in learning about and practicing the methods of Chinese brush painting outlined in this book. The following pages consist of good quality Chinese paper so that you can put into practice some of the techniques you have learned. As the paper is very absorbent, the sheets are perforated and should be removed from the book before you start painting.